More books in the U-Ventures series
Return to the Cave of Time

U-VentureS™

Through the Black Hole

EDWARD PACKARD

Illustrated by DREW WILLIS

SIMON & SCHUSTER BOOKS *for* YOUNG READERS

New York   London   Toronto   Sydney   New Delhi

SIMON & SCHUSTER BOOKS FOR YOUNG READERS
An imprint of Simon & Schuster Children's Publishing Division
1230 Avenue of the Americas, New York, New York 10020
This book is a work of fiction. Any references to historical events, real people, or real locales are used fictitiously. Other names, characters, places, and incidents are products of the author's imagination, and any resemblance to actual events or locales or persons, living or dead, is entirely coincidental.
Text copyright © 1985, 1990, 2010 by Edward Packard
Originally published in 1985 by Bantam Books as the title *Choose Your Own Adventure: Through the Black Hole*
Original books by Edward Packard from the classic Choose Your Own Adventure® series, adapted, revised, and expanded by the author.
Choose Your Own Adventure® is now a registered trademark of Chooseco LLC, which is not associated in any way with U-Ventures, Edward Packard, or Simon & Schuster, Inc.
U-VENTURES is a trademark of Edward Packard.
All rights reserved, including the right of reproduction in whole or in part in any form.
SIMON & SCHUSTER BOOKS FOR YOUNG READERS is a trademark of Simon & Schuster, Inc.
For information about special discounts for bulk purchases, please contact Simon & Schuster Special Sales at 1-866-506-1949 or business@simonandschuster.com.
The Simon & Schuster Speakers Bureau can bring authors to your live event.
For more information or to book an event, contact the Simon & Schuster Speakers Bureau at 1-866-248-3049 or visit our website at www.simonspeakers.com.
Book design by Hilary Zarycky
The text for this book is set in Galliard.
The illustrations for this book are rendered in pen and ink.
Manufactured in the United States of America
0712 OFF
10 9 8 7 6 5 4 3 2 1
This book is catalogued with the Library of Congress.
ISBN 978-1-4424-3426-4
ISBN 978-1-4424-5284-8 (eBook)

Is Travel Through a Black Hole Possible?

Gravity is so strong in the center of a black hole that all matter falling into it is ripped apart by tidal forces and finally crushed into a single point, the "singularity."

That would seem to answer the question. Yet some scientists have speculated that "wormholes" could exist that would connect vastly separated areas of space-time. A wormhole might exist in a black hole.

In his novel, *Contact*, the renowned astronomer Carl Sagan postulated that an advanced civilization could construct such a wormhole. In the movie version the lead character, played by Jodie Foster, travels through a wormhole to a planet of Vega, a bright star twenty-five light-years from Earth. Conceivably, humans might travel through a wormhole to another universe.

Most scientists would say that such a notion is magical, not scientific. But consider: Achievements that would have seemed magical to scientists a few hundred years ago—like nuclear energy and the Internet—now seem commonplace. Achievements that might be commonplace a few hundred years from now would seem magical to us today.

Edward Packard

You've never felt so excited. You just graduated from Space Academy, and you're waiting outside the office of Dr. Andre Bartok, Director of Interstellar Exploration. In a few moments you'll receive your first assignment in space.

You've hardly settled into your chair when an assistant says, "Dr. Bartok will see you now."

The thin, balding director looks up from his computer as you enter the room.

"Come in—I've been expecting you." He smiles for a moment, then gestures for you to take a seat on the other side of his long, crescent-shaped desk. You glance around the luxurious room. A huge montage of the Canopus star system lines one wall. Opposite it is a holographic display screen.

Through the window behind the director's desk you can see the new *Athena* spaceship parked on the tarmac. You hold your breath as you watch Dr. Bartok scanning your file. It seems like forever before he looks up from his screen.

"You've had a brilliant record at the academy," he says, "and I want to send you on a mission of great importance. I'm going to give you a chance to pilot the *Athena*."

You practically fall out of your chair when

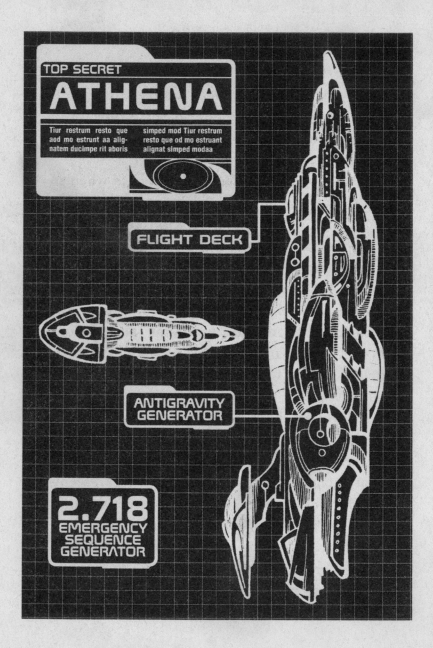

you hear this. Most of your experience has been in simulators and on training cruises. Yet the *Athena* is the most advanced spaceship in the fleet. It has unbelievable speed and maneuvering capability.

"Well," Dr. Bartok says, "are you interested?"

"Interested? I sure am. I can hardly believe it. I would have thought you'd want an older, more experienced astronaut for such a mission."

"You're right. I would," he says with a laugh. Then his face becomes serious. "The reason you have been selected is because you are young. This mission requires long periods of hibernation and two major time dislocations. Our tests show that only someone about your age can withstand the stress involved. If we were to put you into suspended animation when you were ten years older, you might never wake up."

"I understand," you say, though you're beginning to feel a little nervous. "Just what is this mission about, Dr. Bartok? Is it what I've heard rumors of—the first probe of the Pleiades star system?"

The director types a code into his computer.

The room darkens slightly, and a projection of the Milky Way galaxy appears on the holographic screen.

"We have in mind a more important, more daring mission than that," he says. "Nothing less than a trip to another universe. We want to send the *Athena* through MX-12, a black hole near the center of our galaxy."

You sit dumbstruck, thinking of what you learned about black holes at the academy. You know that there are places where matter is squeezed together—where gravity is so great that not even light can escape it, which is why, if you were close enough to see one, it would look absolutely black.

That's frightening enough, but what's worse is that everything that enters a black hole keeps falling until it reaches a point where its entire mass is compressed into nonexistence!

Some scientists have argued that all this mass can't completely disappear—that it has to go somewhere. They believe that in black holes there may be "wormholes" leading to another place, and that astronauts knowing the parameters of a wormhole could navigate through one and survive.

"Excuse me, Dr. Bartok," you say. "Wouldn't tidal forces rip a spaceship to neutrons before it even reached the wormhole?"

The director glances at a document coming out of his printer.

"That's the general rule," he says, "but if the black hole is rotating, and is big enough, it's theoretically possible to get through."

Those words "theoretically possible" bother you. No theory is valid until it's been tested. And no human—not even a supercomputer—knows what happens in a black hole. You're not eager to stake your life on a mere prediction.

Dr. Bartok must see the doubt in your face, because he says, "Of course, you don't have to go on this mission. I wouldn't have called you in except that on your questionnaire you said you were ready for anything. There is another option. We're also going to send the *Athena*'s sister ship, the *Nimrod*, to the edge of the black hole. It will act as a rescue ship and observer. Of course, I must warn you, even going to the edge of a black hole is dangerous. So if you prefer, I'll assign you to the transport service, where you'll be as safe as if you stayed in bed all day."

You don't feel like risking your life getting anywhere near a black hole, but going into the transport service and spending ten years or so carrying iridium crystals back from Vega-9, or something

like that, would be hugely boring. There's no doubt in your mind about what to say:

"I'll accept the assignment, sir."

Dr. Bartok gets up and comes around to shake your hand. "I'm delighted," he says.

"Now, do you choose to go on the observer ship, the *Nimrod*, or are you willing to go on the *Athena* and try to make it through the black hole?"

Go on the Athena, *turn to page 8.*
Go on the Nimrod, *turn to page 31.*

"I'd rather go on the *Athena*," you answer.

Dr. Bartok nods vigorously. "Excellent—I wish I could go with you. If you make it, you may see things that could never be observed on Earth, or even in our galaxy—things that are literally out of this universe. And I have something to tell you that may relieve your anxiety."

"What's that, sir?"

"This is top secret, so not a word about it."

"Of course, sir. You can count on me."

Dr. Bartok walks behind you and closes the door to his office.

"Only a few people know about this," he says. "The *Athena* is equipped with an anti-gravity generator, the first ever to be deployed. Don't try to use it except to escape from the pull of a black hole. There wouldn't be enough gravitational resistance against it. Another thing: It can be operated only once before being recharged back on Earth, so use it only as a last resort."

"Certainly, sir. I hope we don't need it. But another problem is that I've had no training with it."

"You won't need any. All you have to do is remember the emergency code—3.1415. This is

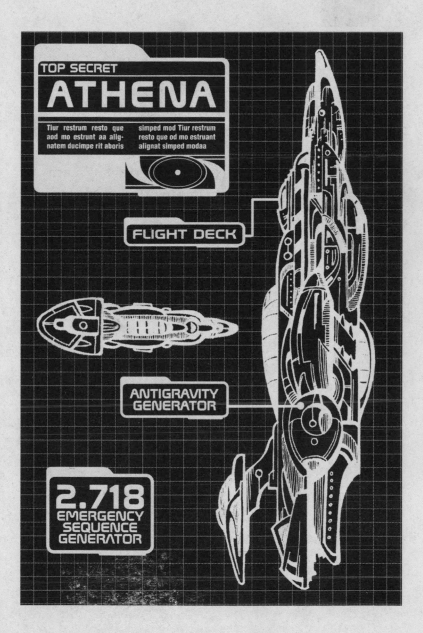

top secret, of course. You are forbidden to write it down. You must remember it."

"Right—3.1415. I won't forget it, sir."

"I'm sure you won't, but I must tell you one more thing. The antigravity generator should work when used in the right circumstances, but we can't guarantee that something won't go wrong."

"What would happen then?"

Dr. Bartok frowns and lowers his voice: "Everything in your spaceship—every part of your body—would fly apart at nearly the speed of light."

"Not a pretty thought, sir."

"I'm afraid not. Now on to a cheerier topic. I'm sure you'll want to know who your copilot will be—Nick Torrey."

What a break—Nick is one of your best friends! "I'm very excited," you say.

You're not only excited, you're scared. If things don't go well, even with an antigravity generator you could end up as trillions of neutrons crushed in the middle of the black hole.

Continue to page 11.

Cape Canaveral—Three Weeks Later

The *Athena* is on the launching pad. You and your copilot, Nick Torrey, are strapped into your positions in the command station.

You've been checked out on the antigravity generator. Your Mark VII celestial computer has passed all tests.

The whole world is tuned to its video screens, watching as the countdown proceeds.

Many have praised your mission as being the most important in history, though some have said that it's a waste of money and will be a waste of your life, too—that no one, ever, can survive a trip through the black hole.

They may be right. But it's too late to change your mind now. A green light flashes on your instrument panel. Final countdown: four, three, two, one . . .

Turn to page 13.

Deep Space—180 Months Later

You and Nick have just awakened from hibernation. The computer didn't disturb you until the *Athena* was only a few billion miles from the black hole.

Nick is bent over a view screen. He looks over at you.

"Hey, you overslept," he says. "I've been up for five minutes."

You laugh politely, swing out of your bunk, and ask the computer for a scan of celestial objects within ten light-years. You know you should be looking for the wormhole parameters—the key that will allow you to pass through the black hole and enter another universe—but you're fixated on data the computer is feeding you.

"Nick, check screen four!" you say. "A terra planet, one almost exactly like early Earth. Its sun is a class G star only two billion years old."

Nick lets out a noise as if he's cheering at a football game.

"This is what NASA has been spending a fortune looking for!"

"Yeah," you agree. "It could be the backup planet we'll need when the sun heats up."

Nick's cheering is replaced by a groan. "We missed the wormhole parameters!"

"Ow. That hurts. My fault," you say. "It will be hard to find the wormhole without them."

"Shall we scratch the black hole mission and inspect the terra planet?" Nick asks.

"Can't. It would violate our orders," you say. At the same time, you're thinking that this would be the wisest thing to do.

Break off the black hole mission and head for the terra planet, continue to page 15.

Continue on to the black hole, turn to page 26.

This terra planet is what every Earth scientist has been hoping to find, a place so like our own planet that humans could settle there.

Scientists are aware that the sun is gradually heating up. This is not the cause of global warming, which has to do with Earth's retaining more of the heat it receives from the sun because of carbon dioxide buildup. The sun itself is heating up as it burns faster. Someday Earth will be too hot for living creatures, no matter what is done about carbon emissions. Long before then, earthlings must find a sister planet that they can colonize. There are billions of planets in our galaxy, but very, very, very few that are like Earth.

It's with this thought in mind that you set course for Terra, the name traditionally given to Earth-like planets. In your opinion, finding a "twin Earth" is more important than trying to get through a black hole.

Within hours good news comes from your computer. Terra's sun is an orange-yellow star with an estimated life of over twelve billion years. The planet's orbit around it is such that it will get approximately the right amount of heat and light for five billion years after Earth becomes uninhabitable!

Terra grows steadily larger in your field of view. Your computer's mapping program shows that it's 65 percent covered by oceans, about the same as Earth. Cloud cover approximates that on Earth. Atmosphere is similar too, except that oxygen content at sea level is what you'd find at an altitude of about six thousand feet on Earth, thinner than at sea level but easy to acclimate to.

A big question is, Does life exist on Terra, and if so, what's it like? You've detected blue-green areas on the planet's continents, but nothing resembling the great rain forests that are still prominent features of Earth, though many of them have been destroyed.

To find out if there is life on Terra, you'll have to set the *Athena* down on its surface.

You order the computer to prepare for landing but get back some bad news: If you use fuel to land on Terra and take off again, you won't have enough to get back to Earth.

From a scientific standpoint your work would still be extremely valuable: You'd be able to radio data to Earth that might save humans from extinction!

Nick tells you that he is willing to land even though it means never getting off the planet again. You're not so sure. The stakes are enormous for humankind, but it's a huge sacrifice to make—committing to spend your life on another planet.

As you're mulling this, an interesting thought occurs to you. You might be able to use the anti-gravity generator to get off Terra's surface. If it works, you'll have more than enough fuel to get back to Earth.

Land on Terra, turn to page 18.

Collect what data you can and set course for Earth, turn to page 22.

The *Athena* passes smoothly through Terra's atmosphere. Your eyes are fixed on the surface, hoping to see signs of plant or animal life.

"There's no pollution," Nick says. "Everything looks clean and fresh. But so far I don't see anything that's alive."

While Nick is talking, you are concentrating on finding a place to land. A few minutes later you set the *Athena* down on a high bluff overlooking a harbor.

You and Nick step out on the bare rock plain. You don't see any signs of life, but the water, clouds, and sky remind you of Earth, except for the slight orange hue caused by the color of Terra's sun. The air smells sweet and clean, though it's a little thin. Air temperature is what you'd expect on a pleasant summer day.

You send out a robot to collect and analyze soil, water, and air samples. It returns half an hour later, and the computer analyzes its findings: Terra is rich in microscopic plant and animal forms with chemistry similar to that found on Earth!

This is great news. It means you'll be able to collect and process enough food. Even though

life has not developed here as much as on Earth, you are confident that Terra will sustain a large human population.

Computer analysis shows that Terra is similar to what Earth was like five hundred million years ago, well before the advent of dinosaurs. The largest animals here are probably not much bigger than ants, but if evolution follows a pattern similar to that experienced on Earth, in a few hundred million years Terra will be rich in large-scale animal and plant life. Trees will likely grow higher than on Earth because Terra's gravity is about 20 percent less.

You're quite sure that some creatures that evolve here will swim, some will fly, and some may even think the way humans do. Some may look like animals you've seen in the zoo.

It's exciting thinking about how life on Terra will develop, but you're feeling depressed. Terra may be Earth-like, but it's not Earth. You don't want to live here. You want to go home!

The computer made it clear that the *Athena* couldn't use fuel to get back into space and still have enough to reach Earth.

You can think of only one possible way to

escape, and that's to use the antigravity generator.

Type in the computer code for the antigravity generator,
turn to page 24.

Resign yourself to staying on Terra,
turn to page 25.

You remember Dr. Bartok's warning not to use the antigravity generator except to escape from a black hole. Instead of enabling you to get back to Earth, it would probably blow you, Nick, and the *Athena* into elementary particles.

Terra looks promising as a colony for humans in the future, but you're not willing to land on it and never be able to get off. You instruct the computer to collect what data it can and set course for Earth; then you and Nick get into your hibernation suits, lie down, and go to sleep.

Years pass. One day the computer awakens you with welcome news: The *Athena* is approaching Earth and will set down on it within the hour.

Much on the ground looks different than you remember, but your ship makes a smooth landing at the space base. Because of relativistic effects, you have aged only a few months over the course of many Earth years. Scientists who were still children when you left Earth help you out of the ship. After medical checks you meet with the head of the Earth Federation and are interviewed by a panel of scientists. When you've finished, the chief scientist of the Earth Federation looks at you intently.

"It's interesting what you found out about

Terra," he says, "but I'm sorry to tell you it's useless knowledge. Terra, along with its sun, is drifting toward the black hole that you were sent to investigate. The rate of movement is constantly increasing. Terra will fall into the black hole and be destroyed within twenty years."

It's a heavy blow to hear this. "Maybe I could go on another mission to the black hole," you say.

"I'm afraid not," the chief scientist says. "As you know, you violated orders by taking the *Athena* to Terra instead of trying to go through the black hole. You will never be allowed on another space mission. We do have a new job for you, though, taking ice core samples in Antarctica."

The End

Too late, you remember that you were never to use the antigravity generator except to escape a black hole.

The End

You remember Dr. Bartok's warning not to use the antigravity generator except to escape from a black hole. You'll just have to make the best of life on Terra and not mope over it. With Nick's help you set up a laser-directed radio transmitter to send information to scientists on Earth. Even traveling at the speed of light, it won't get there for years, but when it arrives, it will be one of the biggest news stories ever.

Once the transmitter is up and operating, you secure the *Athena* so it won't be damaged in a storm, pack up your tools and supplies, and set out to explore this new world.

Who knows what you'll find!

The End

"I'd like to investigate Terra," you tell Nick, "but we'd better stick to the mission we were assigned to—trying to make it through the black hole."

Nick nods, but you can tell he's not happy. You can't blame him. Now that you've missed the wormhole parameters, the chances of getting through are close to zero.

But you have no time to dwell on such thoughts. The *Athena* is nearing the event horizon. You have to be ready for any emergency, and sooner or later an emergency is bound to happen.

It happens sooner! The computer screen lights up, telling of something that you studied at the academy but never thought you'd experience:

Gravitational field anomaly.

Nick's eyes are on the screen.

"What's that?"

"I studied this at the academy," you say. "It's not exactly good news, but it could give us the chance we need to ride a gravity wave through the wormhole."

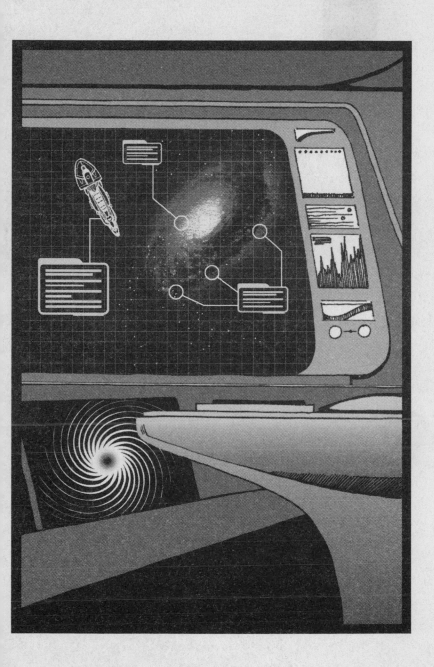

Even as you're saying this, you're thinking that latching on to a gravity wave is an extremely delicate procedure. The slightest error in speed, course, timing, or acceleration would be fatal.

*Try to latch on to a gravity wave,
continue to page 29.*

Try to think of something else, turn to page 30.

You concentrate on detecting a newly forming gravity wave. Nick slows the *Athena* to give you more time.

A few minutes later the computer reports that it has identified a weak wave. There is a low probability that it could carry you through.

Attempt to ride the wave you detected,
turn to page 86.

Wait in hopes of detecting a stronger gravity wave,
turn to page 33.

You're still trying to think of what to do when the screen lights up.

Gravitational field anomaly stabilized.

Is that good or bad? Your mind feels numbed by stress. None of your training has prepared you for this.

Stop feeling pathetic! you tell yourself. You've got to think what to do.

Meanwhile, the computer monitor shows that the *Athena* is gathering tremendous speed, heading straight for the center of the black hole.

Another message comes up.

Thruster sensor failure!

Try to get safely through, turn to page 79.

Try to reverse course and return to Earth, turn to page 80.

You're in command of the spaceship *Nimrod* and just woke up from hibernation. Your mission is to observe your sister ship, the *Athena*, as it attempts to pass through the black hole and to be of assistance in any way you can. You and your crewmate, Kate Soeiro, are trying to stay as close to the *Athena* as possible in case of trouble.

The stars behind you appear as reddish, glowing clusters because of the effects of relativity. You're traveling almost as fast as the *Athena*, but you're having difficulty staying in contact with it because of magnetic forces surrounding the black hole. Now a faint message has come through—a call for help: The *Athena*'s main thrusters have failed!

You set course for the other ship at maximum speed.

"How close to the black hole can we get?" you ask Kate.

She's already keying data into the computer, and asks it:

"What chance have we of rescuing the crew of the *Athena*?"

The answer comes back:

Chance of rescuing Athena *crew and escaping black hole: 22%.*
Chance of failing to rescue Athena *crew and escaping black hole: 18%.*
Chance of being swept into black hole along with Athena *crew: 41%.*
Variability factor—no prediction possible: 19%.

"There you have it," Kate says. "What shall we do?"

Try to rescue the Athena *crew, turn to page 34.*
Decide it's too risky, turn to page 42.

You keep trying, directing and redirecting the computer, but have no success detecting a stronger gravity wave.

Meanwhile, the *Athena* has been drifting closer to the center. The weak gravity wave passes. You and Nick look at each other. Neither of you knows what to do. Buzzers sound. Flashing lights come on. The *Athena* is accelerating, spiraling downward. Seconds later it's destroyed by tidal forces near the center of the black hole. . . .

The End

"We can't just leave them, Kate. Let's go for it."

"Agreed," she says.

You're already keying instructions into the computer. The *Nimrod* begins speeding toward the other ship. You radio the *Athena*'s crew that you're coming, though it's unlikely the message will get through. The magnetic field near a black hole turns radio waves into a jumble. You're straining the *Nimrod*'s space drive to the maximum, trying to reach the *Athena* before both ships slip below the event horizon—the point of no return. You ask the computer for the latest probability profile. The words appear on the screen:

Chance of rescuing the Athena*: 0%.*

"Kate, look at the computer!"

Her face is ashen. "But . . . why?"

You're already asking the same question. In a moment you get the answer:

Athena *destroyed by tidal forces at the periphery of the black hole.*

You have failed to rescue the crew of the *Athena*, and the *Nimrod* itself is in peril. You command the computer to execute escape maneuvers, but get another message instead:

Passing through the event horizon.

"There's no turning back now," Kate says. Suddenly your mission has changed. Instead of being the observers, you and Kate are the ones who must try to make it through the black hole! The only trouble is that you haven't been maneuvering in the precise way necessary to enter the wormhole.

The *Nimrod* is creaking and groaning from the gravitational differential between the bow and the stern. Even your body is being stretched! Gravity is so intense that the part of you nearest the black hole is falling faster than the part farthest from it! You hear Kate's voice, croaking, as if her vocal cords are strained to the breaking point:

"I've put the computer on autopilot and told it to get us into the wormhole," she says.

You're both pinned against your restraints as the computer adjusts course. The scene through the view port is indescribably weird. Behind you is nothing but a faint red glow. Ahead, space is completely black, except for a ghostly halo of dark violet. In the center of the halo is the singularity, the source of the terrifying gravitational field that is probably about to crush you.

Unlike the *Athena*, the *Nimrod* isn't equipped with an antigravity generator. Your only hope is that some unknown force is at work near the center of the hole, a force that could lead you to another universe!

Your fingers are shaking as you punch a question into the computer: "Can you steer us into the wormhole?"

The reply comes back:

Quantum divergence.

You know what that means: The normal laws of physics do not apply here. Neither logic nor knowledge will help you decide.

Kate is also watching. "I thought it might come to this," she says softly.

You sit frozen at the controls. How can you make a decision if you have no reason to do anything?

Turn to either page 56 or page 50.

"You make the repair, Nick," you say.

Without a word, he puts on his space suit, grabs the kit with sealant XK42, and steps into the air lock. In a moment the hatch closes behind him.

The seconds tick by.

It's hard waiting. What's going on out there? You feel panic building. You want to help, but there's nothing you can do.

Time is running out!

"Nick! Nick! Are you all right? What's going on? Can you hear me?"

Turn to page 38.

Nick's voice: "Mission accomplished—no problem."

No problem! That's Nick—real cool about everything. At least most of the time.

"Good going," you say. "Now get back in here. We have another problem ahead—the biggest black hole in the galaxy!"

You wait anxiously for him to reach the hatch and let himself in. You touch a few keys on your computer keyboard. The screen displays the information you want:

Distance to event horizon:
14,640,880,000 miles.
Distance to singularity: 14,822,000,000 miles
Speed: .54 c.

A shudder runs through your body. You can survive inside the event horizon. The singularity is another matter. It is the point at the center where all matter may be crushed out of existence. The numbers on the screen make the black hole sound far away, but .54 c means you're traveling at more than half the speed of light! You didn't realize you were this close to the event horizon. Once you pass it, there will be no chance of

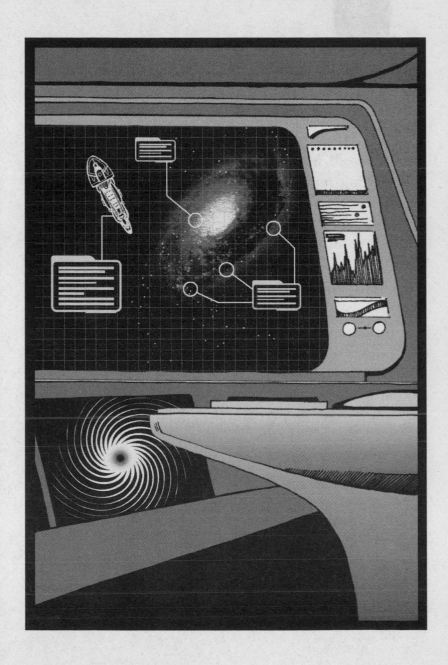

reversing course, even at full emergency power. But where is Nick? You hear his voice:

"I can't open the hatch. It's jammed!"

"Hold on!" Why would the hatch be jammed? Maybe it's relativistic effects. They're getting more extreme every second! You can't leave Nick outside the spaceship while you're entering a black hole.

You've got to get the hatch open, and fast! You rush to activate the electronic controls. They aren't functioning. You try the emergency levers. They won't move. The metal is bent. You turn to the computer and say, "Hatch is inoperable. Metal warped by effects near black hole. What is best action?" You wait for the computer to respond. You're not even sure it's programmed for the solution. At last a response:

Hatch opens inward. Apply 600 pounds pressure evenly against exterior of hatch surface and it will open.

That's no help! There's no way you or Nick could apply such pressure!

"Computer, what is the best way to apply pressure?"

You have to wait for what seems like forever for the reply:

Inertial force.

You almost scream with frustration. Why is the computer being so slow and unhelpful? It's supposed to be the best onboard computer ever built.

You don't have time to ask more questions. You've got to use the computer in your brain! Suddenly you realize how you could use your inertial force to open the hatch. All you have to do is adjust course slightly, and the door will fly open. The question is: In which direction should you turn the ship? The door is on the starboard, or right, side and opens inward. Should you turn the *Athena* slightly to port, or left, or slightly to starboard?

Adjust course to starboard, turn to page 52.
Adjust course to port, turn to page 59.

"The odds are too much against us," you tell Kate. "We'd be pulled into the black hole after the *Athena*. I think we'd better return to the base." You start keying in the coordinates for the return flight to Earth.

"At least we'll have gathered new data on black holes," you say. The booster thrusters fire. The *Nimrod* swings into its new course. Your eyes remain fixed on the deep reddish glow that surrounds the black hole.

You can't get your mind off the astronauts who were crushed into nothingness. You glance over at Kate. She seems hypnotized by the sight as much as you are. Neither of you are looking at the display screen of the area ahead of you. It's not until an audio warning sounds that you're aware of the stray comet hurtling across your path on its way into the black hole.

Normally, you would still have plenty of time to avoid it, but the tremendous gravity of the black hole has accelerated the comet to more than a tenth of the speed of light.

When you become aware of it, it's more than ten thousand miles away, but it travels that far in less than a second.

The End

"I'll make the repair," you say. You put on your space helmet, lock it onto your space suit, grab the kit with XK42, and step inside the air lock. A green light tells you it's safe to proceed.

You open the outer hatch, snap on your tether, and swing into space. Your legs float straight out as you grab the EV rail and move hand-over-hand toward position A-7.

In the sky ahead of you is a coal-black disk, growing larger as you watch.

The computer is patched into the radio in your helmet. You can hear the seconds ticking off. *Thirty-six, thirty-five, thirty-four, thirty-three . . .*

It could take a lot of that time just to reach position A-7, and will take more time to seal the crack.

You give the jet pack on your space suit a burst of power and overshoot, but manage to work your way back along the hull. Finally you reach A-7. The crack is clearly visible. You can almost see it growing!

You get out sealant XK42 and struggle to unscrew the cap.

Why didn't they design it so you could get at it fast?

Finally you get it open.
You apply the sealant!

Continue to page 45.

Sealant XK42 may be hard to open, but it's a miracle of chemistry. The seal you just made is stronger than the original titanium!

Time to get back inside the ship!

You work your way to the hatch, listening to the seconds still ticking in your helmet. The time to failure that the computer predicted is past. What a relief! It was the sensor that was faulty, not the sealant you applied. You reach the outer hatch and look around. The part of the sky where you're headed is a vast black disk. Surrounding it and extending 180 degrees behind you is a shimmering ring of scarlet light.

Nick's voice in your earphones: "You did a great job, but get back in here. We're coming up on the event horizon—traveling at sixty percent of light speed!"

You feel dizzy. The whole ship is vibrating. You're at the edge of the whirlpool, the point from which nothing can return!

Seconds later all is calm again. Your dizziness passes.

You send the radio signal that should open the door. Nothing happens. You try again. Still nothing. Vibrations must have knocked the microlocks out of alignment—you'll have to open it by hand.

"What's the matter?" Nick yells in your earphones. "Are you having—" His voice cuts out.

"Nick?"

No reply.

You struggle with a spanner wrench, trying to loosen the door. Your hands are shaking.

Suddenly the hatch opens—*too much*! It's jammed open. No way you can close it.

You're in the air lock now, but there's no reasonable way you can get inside the cabin—the inner door is designed not to open unless the outer door is closed. You could blast it open, but then the cabin would be depressurized and all the oxygen would escape.

You shout into your mike, "Nick, can you hear me?"

No answer.

You're trapped in space with a half hour of oxygen left, and you can't even talk to Nick! You look around helplessly. The sky is coal black. You have never felt so alone. You don't even have stars to keep you company.

A space traveler is used to stars and galaxies shining far more brightly than they appear on Earth. But now that you're inside the event horizon of a black hole, you and Nick are cut

off—not only from other humans, but from the rest of the universe!

You try Nick again on the radio. Still no luck. You rap on the door. He should be able to hear it. You rap again as loudly as you can and keep rapping.

Then you wait. There's no response. What's wrong with him? Is he still alive? You try to take stock of the situation.

You're inside the radius from which not even light can escape. No telescope on Earth or in outer space could see you, no matter how powerful it was. You are still millions of miles from the singularity, in which matter is crushed out of existence, but you're falling toward that point at more than half the speed of light. You could reach it in less than a minute.

If the rules of physics hold true, you'll have no chance of survival. But some scientists have said that the rules of physics don't apply in a black hole, that no law can describe what happens in such a strong gravity field.

Theories are one thing, but your chances of survival can't be good—you're not even inside your spaceship! You've got to do something!

Why hasn't Nick heard you? He may need

your help. Maybe you should blast the door open. It would depressurize the cabin, and that could hurt Nick, if he is still alive. You weigh the risks for a moment.

Blast the door open, turn to page 60.
Try to think of something better, turn to page 61.

Scientists on Earth have thought up many theories about what it would be like in a massive black hole. Most think that you would be torn apart by a gravity field millions of times stronger than that on Earth. But some say that if the black hole were rotating and you entered at just the right speed and angle, centrifugal force would balance gravitational force, and you might safely pass through.

Sometimes such theories are right, sometimes wrong, and sometimes half right and half wrong. You and Kate are about to find out, for the *Nimrod* is plunging at almost light speed toward the singularity—the terrible vortex.

One thing soon becomes clear and gives you hope. The hole you're falling into is rotating, and the centrifugal force that has been set up precisely balances the force of gravity.

Gradually, like a speck in a column of water swirling around and around on its way down a drain, the *Nimrod* begins to whirl around the vortex.

Turbulence might jostle a speck away from the wall of water, causing it to fall straight down. But this does not happen to the *Nimrod*, which will whirl around the black hole for thousands, and hundreds of thousands, and hundreds of millions of years, at which time, through another quantum divergence, your skeleton, and Kate's, will finally make it through the black hole.

The End

You put on your helmet and command the computer to fire a minimal burst from the port thruster. The *Athena* turns very slightly to the right. At this speed even a slight change produces an inertial force of more than three g's. You're thrown hard against your restraints.

The outer and inner hatches both open, and Nick flies into the main cabin, landing on the inside wall of the hull, his spring-loaded space boots absorbing the shock. Air in the cabin rushes out through the open hatches. Nick floats wildly around, coming to rest only when he grabs the handholds near the air lock.

You hear his voice on the radio in your helmet.

"Thanks for getting me in here. I'll get this hatch shut so we can repressurize."

"Okay," you answer as you adjust the ship back on course. "Let me know if you can use some help."

Even as you're speaking, you can see that no help will be enough. The force from the course correction was so strong it not only forced the inner hatch open, it ripped it from its hinges. It floats by, and you catch it and tie it down.

Nick kicks off a wall and floats to his control

station a few feet away. Neither of you says anything. You both know that you're in deep trouble.
It's dangerous enough trying to get through a
black hole under perfect conditions. To try it now
would be suicide.

Nick has already asked the computer what
options are available.

The answer comes up on the screen:

*Option 1: Reverse course, full power; radio contact
with* Nimrod *may be possible in 13.6 hours.*

*Option 2: Set course for planet Nicron, full
power.*

No other options.

You and Nick exchange glances. "What do
you think?" you ask. "Shall we ask what the per-
centage chance is on each option?"

Nick shakes his head. "Too many variables. We
don't know where the *Nimrod* is. It may be on
its way back to base. As for the planet Nicron . . .
all we know is that it's the nearest one in the Tau
Gamma system."

You glance at the chronometer. You're almost

at the event horizon of the hole, the point beyond which nothing can escape!

Reverse course, turn to page 76.
Try to reach the planet Nicron, turn to page 95.

The *Nimrod*, with you and Kate aboard it, plunges toward the singularity. To your amazement, the computer tells you that the centrifugal force almost precisely matches the gravitational force. You and Kate are not torn apart by gravity, but float weightlessly as the *Nimrod* whirls around and around the vortex of the hole.

The forces here are so great that the mighty thrusters of the *Nimrod* have no effect. There is a chance, though a slight one, that a quantum fluctuation—some unpredictable disturbance—will save you. Normally, the chances of such a thing happening are one in trillions. But inside a black hole, forces are so great that the laws of physics are altered in ways never experienced on Earth.

Without warning, a quantum disturbance flicks the *Nimrod* out of the whirlpool. Exactly what happens then, you'll never know, nor would scientists be able to explain. The forces are so great that you lose consciousness. But when you come to, you know that you must have passed safely to the other side of the black hole, for things are very different than they were before.

Everywhere you look there are stars and

nebulae. Training your telescope on the heavens, you can make out fuzzy patches of light. Most of these, when you increase the magnification, have a familiar spiral pattern.

"If we're in another universe, it's a lot like our own," you say to Kate. "What's more, we seem to be in a galaxy similar to the Milky Way."

Kate looks at you curiously. "Is it possible that after passing through the black hole, we came back to our galaxy?"

"This is a problem for the computer," you say. "It should be able to tell us."

The computer has to analyze the positions of thousands of stars and other galaxies. Fast as it is, it takes almost ten minutes to respond.

Galaxies are close to the positions they were in, but stars are in different positions.

Nothing else shows on the screen, but an amber light indicates that the computer is working on a more precise analysis.

"What do you think of what it's telling us?" Kate asks.

"It's pretty clear," you say. "We're in the same galaxy, but not at the same time—we've come out thousands of years in the past or thousands of years in the future."

As you finish saying this, the computer confirms your guess:

Time is 6,810 years ahead of when you left Earth.

"If that's so," Kate says, "why are the other galaxies still pretty much where they were before?"

"If you'll remember how far away they are, then you'll know," you say. "It's as if you were in a car going fifty miles an hour and closed your eyes for a few seconds. When you opened them, nearby trees and houses would be in a different direction than when you last looked, but distant mountains would still be in the same direction."

As you say this, you're punching instructions into the computer: "Locate Earth and sun. Set course to intercept them. Give estimated time of arrival."

Fortunately, the sun and Earth are close by— only a few hundred light-years away. You and Kate settle down for a long hibernation. When you wake up, you'll be home, almost ten thousand years after you left. You go to sleep, dreaming what it will be like.

The End

Adjusting course to port, you command the computer to fire a minimal burst from the starboard thruster.

This causes the ship to turn slightly to the left. At this speed even a very slight course change produces an inertial force of more than three g's! You're thrown hard against your restraints. It hurts. But what hurts more is realizing that the hatch has not only opened; it has flown off into space and taken Nick with it!

You instruct the computer to compensate for the variation, but you can already feel the opening in the hull, then nothing, as the *Athena* is ripped apart.

The End

You pull out your laser pistol, aim it at the latch, and squeeze the trigger. An arrow of light streaks out, but instead of being a straight beam, it's bent in an arc, curving back toward the stern of the ship, where liquid hydrogen is stored. *How could that have happened?*

Suddenly you realize why: You're traveling at almost the speed of light in a massive gravitational field. Of course the laser's ray would be bent!

The liquid hydrogen explodes in a weirdly distorted flare of light. The blast tears the *Athena*, Nick, and you into molecules that are soon reduced to neutrons that disappear completely when they reach the singularity—the center of the black hole.

The End

You're desperate, but you can't see anything to be gained by blasting the door open. If Nick is still alive, he'd lose all his oxygen and could be hurt by depressurization.

But what else can you do? You're traveling at close to the speed of light. Within a minute you could reach the singularity, where all matter falling into the black hole is compressed to a geometrical point. How this can happen is a paradox—a situation that seems impossible but isn't.

This is no time to speculate. You work your way along the EV rail, moving forward, away from the thrusters. You reach the starboard view port of the control station and look inside.

Nick is slumped in his seat. There's a dark reddish spot in his hair—blood. He's still breathing. He must have been knocked unconscious by some object when the ship passed through the event horizon.

You take a wrench from your tool kit and rap on the cabin view port. Nick stirs a little. You beat out the Mayday signal. You hit the view port so hard it would break if it weren't made of meteorite-resistant glass.

Nick stirs again. He lifts his head. You keep

rapping. He looks around. He sees you. Slowly he staggers to his feet and motions toward the hatch. He's going to open it! Luckily, he still has his earphones on.

"Nick!" you yell into your mike. "The outer hatch is blown off. You have to depressurize before opening."

He nods and puts on his helmet. All is silent. You relax a little. He's depressurizing the cabin slowly—compressing the cabin's air into a tank so that loose objects won't be blown out when he opens the hatch.

He opens the hatch and lets you inside.

"I don't know what hit me," he says.

"Turbulence when we crossed the event horizon."

Nick looks out. "I don't see any stars."

You shake your head. "We're cut off from the rest of the universe."

Nick looks at the chronometer. "We must be almost at the—"

"Singularity," you complete his thought. "Got to get ready fast! Computer: Repressurize the cabin."

It takes a few more seconds to secure yourself for what's to come.

It begins as a little shuddering of the ship. Not the ordinary kind of turbulence—just a slight quivering. This motion stops, and everything is frozen. The clock has stopped. You know this because you're staring at it. You can't stop staring at it. You can't look anywhere else. You can't move a muscle. Not even your eyeballs. You can't blink. You can't breathe, either, yet you don't need air. Nick must be in the same situation, though you can't see him—you're facing the other way.

Even stranger is the way you feel, as if you are in a dream, though you know you're awake. You wonder if time itself has stopped and you'll be frozen like this forever.

You can't move, but you can feel, and you have never felt such hopelessness, such despair. Better to have been crushed in a black hole than to be trapped in time, doomed to sit for eternity, staring at a stopped clock.

Years seem to pass, though it may only be days or hours or seconds—you'll never know. And nothing has changed except that you have slowly become aware that you are in total darkness. The lights in your spaceship have either gone out or you have gone blind. You can't tell because you can't move.

If you could only report back to Earth what

has happened. It would be of great interest to scientists to learn that a spaceship sent into a massive black hole will not necessarily be torn apart or crushed, that it may simply become suspended in time. But of course you'll never be able to tell anyone. Even if you could move enough to work the radio, no signal could escape.

If only you could talk to Nick. Perhaps you can reach him through mental telepathy. *Nick . . . Nick . . . can you hear my thoughts?*

It's no use. The harder you try, the more your mind freezes.

For a moment you think that you might sleep, but you're unable to do even that. You can only sit motionless, waiting for that which may never come.

Turn to page 66.

You're not sure how much time has passed. You first think that you're back home in your own bed, then that you're in the hospital. But it is not a doctor standing by your bunk, it's Nick smiling down at you.

"I'm glad you came out of it, pal—I've only been awake a few minutes, but I was feeling pretty lonely."

You sit up and look around, rubbing your eyes. Only then do you remember that you're inside the *Athena* and that when you lost consciousness you were falling into a black hole and time had seemed to stop.

You look through the view port. The sky isn't black; it's a sort of pleasing apple green.

"Nick, did we make it?"

He nods. "We're on the other side." His voice is really soft, as if the two of you entered a tomb or a great cathedral. You know he feels the way you do—filled with awe.

There's something about the light that makes you feel different, like you're in a place beyond space and time. That, of course, is what's happened. You have entered another universe.

You glance at the status screen. It reads:

Course: undeterminable. Speed: infinity.

"Nick, I don't care if we have entered another universe—we can't be traveling at infinite speed."

"I don't think we are," he says, "but we may be traveling faster than light speed in our own universe. The computer would register that as infinity."

"So the laws of physics are different in this universe," you say.

"Some of them must be," Nick says. "That could help us or it could hurt us."

You stare out of first one view port and then another. Everywhere you look is the same vaporous apple green color, except for directly behind the spaceship, where you can make out a small white patch in the sky.

"Is that where we came from?" you ask.

"I think so. I've been keeping an eye on it since I woke up. It's getting smaller by the minute."

"So on this side the black hole is white!"

"We've learned that much, at least," says Nick. "And that in this universe, space must be filled with some luminous gas; otherwise, it would look black, the way it does in our universe."

"But if it were filled with gas, then we'd be slowing down and heating up, the way we do when we enter a planet's atmosphere."

Nick looks at you for a moment, thinking, then says, "That would be true unless the gas is extremely thin."

He punches keys on the computer. In a moment he reports, "Our sensors can't identify what's around us."

"I guess that's because of the different laws of physics here."

"We may never find out what the laws are," Nick says. "Our sensors show nothing, except that we're traveling at infinite speed."

"Let's see if the ship can still maneuver."

You instruct the computer to first increase and then decrease power, then to turn at various angles. Everything works, but very sluggishly, or maybe time is moving at an extremely slow rate.

"At some point we may want to get back home," Nick says. "Let's turn around and head toward the black hole—I mean, the white hole. I want to see if we can get closer to it."

"Let's think a second, Nick," you say. "If we can get back to our own universe, and to Earth, and report what we've experienced, it would be a tremendous accomplishment, but it would be even greater if we could learn more about this universe. Does it have stars and planets, for instance?"

"It would be nice to see more of it," says Nick. "But the farther we go and the more fuel we spend, the less likely it is we'll ever get back. Well, it's your decision."

Turn the Athena *around and try to get back to your own universe, turn to page 70.*

Continue on in the new universe, turn to page 74.

In a second or two you've given the computer all the instructions it needs.

Slowly—very slowly—the *Athena* turns back toward the fuzzy white patch that is probably the only link to your universe.

It takes almost an hour before you can completely reverse course. Your instruments still indicate the *Athena* is doing the impossible—traveling at infinite speed—so you have no idea what your speed really is.

Your eyes are fixed on the forward view port. You should see the white hole getting larger as you get closer. But it's not—it's getting smaller, as if you are still heading away from it!

Nick works on figuring out an explanation. At last he reports, "Our computer says the data won't compute."

"I'm afraid it's almost useless in this universe," you say. "All I can think of is that we're in some kind of gaseous flow that's carrying us along with it, away from the white hole. The current is so strong we can't make headway against it."

"Let's turn back the other way," Nick says. "At least then we'll be pointed in the direction we're moving."

It takes another hour to bring your ship back on its original course. By this time the fuzzy white patch is completely out of sight.

Nick sighs. "I guess we're stuck in this universe."

"Worse than that," you say. "We're going to starve, if we don't run out of oxygen first."

"Look!" Nick points ahead and a little to the right of the ship. A round, grayish shape—what seems to be a planet—is growing larger as you get closer to it. Soon you see others. They come in different sizes, but each of them looks as smooth as a billiard ball.

"I don't think they would support human life," Nick says.

"Probably not, but let's get as close a look as we can."

The *Athena* speeds by several of the smooth gray planets. You see one that appears to be about the size of Earth. You point to it on the screen. "Let's head for it."

Nick gives a thumbs-up.

"I'm swinging her now," he says. "I'll put braking thrusters on standby—we don't know how strong the gravity will be in this universe."

"Good thinking," you say. But you soon see

that gravity isn't going to be a problem. Your rate of approach keeps slowing, even as you apply more power!

Nick is staring at the instruments. "This is incredible. It's as if gravity is working backward by pushing us away!"

"Of course—that's it!" you exclaim. "That's why we couldn't get back to the white hole—it was repulsing us."

"This is a disaster," Nick says. "How can we land on a planet here? The moment we turn off the power, we'll catapult back into space."

"There's one possibility," you say. "If by some chance this planet is hollow and we could get inside it, then we could walk around on the inside of the shell—like ants crawling on the inside of a hollowed-out pumpkin."

"Maybe so," Nick says. "But what makes you think a planet might be hollow? There aren't any hollow planets in our universe!"

"That's because of gravity," you say. "But here we're seeing reverse gravity, which could hollow out the middle of the sphere as all the material in it is repulsed up to the planet's inner surface."

"How could we get to the planet's inner surface? There are no signs of any cracks or holes."

"It looks like a rather soft material to me," you say. "If we hit the surface at full power, we might be able to burrow in. This ship is designed to take heavy shocks."

Nick shakes his head. "Sounds like suicide."

"It would be in our universe, but I don't think it will be here."

You take a look out the view port at endless green space. It seems empty of everything but smooth, gray planets.

"Well," you say, "we could just keep cruising along and hope to find something else, but wherever we go, we'll have the same problem of reverse gravity. Our food and oxygen won't last forever."

Nick stares out the view port, straining to see something else, perhaps a planet more like Earth.

Finally he says, "It's up to you, friend."

Try to hit the gray planet at full speed and burrow in, turn to page 98.

Keep cruising, hoping to find something else, turn to page 101.

"Let's see what we can find in this universe," you say. At the same time you accelerate the thrusters. The *Athena* streaks on through vaporous green space. You strain your eyes and keep checking the display screen, looking for stars or planets that might lie ahead.

"There's one, off to the side," says Nick. "Edis eht ot ffo, eno s'ereht."

Huh? He's talking gibberish. What's going on? You look at the instruments. Somehow the *Athena* is going backward! And, listening to Nick, you realize that he is talking backward! The same thing happens when you try to speak.

The controls are all indicating the opposite of what they should. Distance is decreasing back to the white hole that is this universe's side of the black hole in your own universe.

Now you're lying in the position you were in when you came out of the white hole. You feel the shuddering and violent dislocation as you go back into it. You wonder if time will keep running backward once you're in your own universe.

It doesn't. The shuddering stops. You're not back in your own universe. You have gone through a different wormhole—one that leads not to your universe, but to one where forward- and backward-moving time are perfectly balanced. Time is no longer passing.

The End

You instruct the computer to reverse course and seek out the *Nimrod*. You know you are close to the point of no return. Still, you're not prepared for the g-forces as the computer orders maximum power to bring the *Athena* on its new course. The gravitational force in the vicinity of a black hole is incredibly great.

Only a supremely advanced space drive like the *Athena*'s could break such a grip.

The ship turns ever so slowly, following an arc through space tens of thousands of miles long. At the crest of the arc—the point where you're closest to the black hole and the gravitational force is the strongest—the ship seems to hover, as if it can't decide which force to yield to. The slightest loss of power means certain destruction.

Slowly at first, then faster, the distance to the black hole begins to lengthen.

You hear Nick's voice in your speaker. "I think we're going to make it."

Nine hours have passed since you escaped from the gravitational field of the black hole. Your radar is functioning again. Nick is scanning the area where the *Nimrod* should be on station.

He's still trying when you pick up something on the radio. It's coming from a beamer, a missile containing a radio that beams a recorded message. The repeating message is encrypted. You instruct the computer to decipher it, then tell Nick to look at the monitor. The message is coming up:

To Athena *from* Nimrod: *Mayday. Mayday. We lost power in our main thrusters. We are being pulled into the black hole. By the time you receive . . . we'll be gone. Good luck, mates. Farewell.*

The *Athena* may be lost too: There's no chance of getting on the precise course that will get the ship through the black hole.

"We don't have enough fuel or oxygen now to reach home base," Nick says, "or even to go to Nicron."

"I'll ask the computer what our options are," you say.

It seems like forever, but in only a few seconds the answer appears:

No options.

"Well," Nick says, "we have to hope the computer is wrong. Maybe we should start for home and hope that another spaceship is cruising in the area."

"I guess so, unless we want to try to make it through the black hole."

"Either way seems hopeless," Nick says.

You shrug. You have to agree with him. And as if you weren't having enough trouble, your space suit isn't working right. It feels like a steam bath inside.

Cruise toward home for as long as you can, turn to page 108.

Try to head the Athena *back toward the black hole, turn to page 143.*

You direct the computer to hold course. Now you and Nick are sitting grim-faced at your terminals, expecting the worst.

A buzzer goes off. Nick's screen lights up.

"Not another failed sensor?"

"I'm afraid so," Nick says. "We still might catch a gravity wave using all our power, but . . ."

"What?"

"There are incredible forces. We'll be trapped if we don't act fast."

Nick sounds like the stress is getting to him.

"We've got to act fast, but we've got to think it through," you say. "We might try to go into the black hole faster than the stuff being pulled in. That way we might keep control of our spaceship. . . . Or we could hold off until we can ride through on a gravity wave."

"If one comes," says Nick.

You've got to decide now!

Hold off and hope you can ride in on a gravity wave,
turn to page 82.

Accelerate at full speed into the black hole,
turn to page 84.

You decide that it would be foolhardy to try to pass through the black hole without knowing the wormhole parameters. You've got to reverse course, and you've got to do it now! You key instructions into the computer.

It's a strain on the *Athena*, and on you and Nick as well, but the ship slowly turns, wavering at times as the force of the black hole pulls on it, finally settling on course for Earth.

You're traveling at two million miles per hour. That sounds fast, but at this speed it will take 116 years to reach Earth.

You try to keep your voice from shaking. "Nick. How long can we stay in hibernation and still survive?"

"There's no way of knowing. But the computer is programmed to wake us up if our lives are in danger."

"That doesn't tell us much," you say. "It could be a hundred and sixteen years from now, or it could be in a few months. We won't age while we're in hibernation, but we will when we come out. If the computer wakes us up in only a few years, we'll die of old age before we reach Earth."

"All we can do is hope," says Nick.

There's nothing to add to that. The two of you get in your hibernation capsules and go to sleep.

Hibernation goes exactly as you hoped. The computer doesn't awaken you and Nick until you're within a few hundred thousand miles of Earth. You check your position and radio NASA, requesting permission to land. No response comes back.

That's troubling, but even more troubling is that the Earth is almost completely covered with clouds.

"What's wrong?" you practically scream at the computer. The whole planet couldn't have clouded over in only 116 years.

The explanation comes back. Far more than 116 years have passed in Earth time. Because you were traveling in the vicinity of a black hole, time slowed for you, but it didn't for Earth and everyone on it. It's now 2360. NASA no longer exists. Ever since Earth clouded over and no one could see stars or planets anymore, humans lost interest in space.

You may find a place to land and people to talk to about your trip. But will you find someone who understands what you're talking about?

The End

You apply reverse thrusters, slowing descent into the hole, but almost immediately you get conflicting signals. Your body is wrenched as if you were in a giant washing machine.

"I don't get it, Nick." Your voice is trembling. "What's happening to us?"

The *Athena* is in the grip of swirling spacetime. Nick reports:

"The computer says we're moving and we're not moving!"

"What you say makes no sense. But what's happening makes no sense! It's as if we're moving, but the space we're in is moving too, so we can't get anywhere."

"I don't understand," Nick wails.

"It's like an eddy in a fast-flowing river, where the current whirls you and won't let go."

"Are we stuck here forever?"

"I don't know. Time may have stopped."

"What?"

"That's what the computer readout means. Time has stopped."

"So that's what happens in a black hole?"

"Can happen. At least we won't be getting any older."

"That's all the worse," says Nick. "We could

be here years, centuries! I can't imagine anything worse."

You try to look for a bright side to the picture, and you will be trying forever.

The End

You apply full power, trying to get through the black hole before you're crushed. Stars and nebulae clustered behind you have taken on an unearthly pale orange glow. The stars ahead have a deep purplish hue. In the center of them is a coal-black disk—the black hole itself.

"It's eerie," Nick says softly. "That black disk is expanding even as we look at it—taking up more space ahead of us."

"We'll soon be surrounded by blackness but won't yet be in a wormhole," you say.

A buzzer sounds.

Nick's face loses its color. A major malfunction has occurred.

"Why did this happen now?"

You ask the computer for details. Your eyes are on the monitor.

"Come on, we need information!"

Exterior hull crack, position A-7: Condition progressive; apply sealant XK42. Time to irreversibility: 48 seconds.

You don't have to talk to Nick about what this means—you've been trained for any emergency. Someone will have to go outside the spaceship and apply sealant at position A-7 before the clock runs out. If the computer is right, the hull is going to split open incredibly soon.

"Will you do it? Maybe I should," Nick says.

The answer doesn't depend on how brave you are—it depends on who can fix the crack faster. You're more athletic than Nick. You're sure you could get in position faster; but he has more of a knack with mechanical things.

Make the repair yourself, turn to page 43.
Tell Nick to make the repair, turn to page 37.

You apply full power, setting up violent vibrations. You're passing through a wormhole. A strong shock. You're passing . . . passing . . . through . . . sned . . . jbumbld . . . t
ACHHCH!

Quantum divergence.

Continue to page 87 or turn to page 88.

All is calm. The sky in all directions is green, not black. No stars or galaxies are in sight.

"Nick!"

"Yes, I'm still here. We . . . we must be in another universe."

As he is speaking, a white cloud, seeming to come from nowhere, appears in front of you. It's approaching, filling up an even larger portion of the sky. In seconds, white fog surrounds you.

"Weird, what is happening, and the way it came after us," says Nick. "I think it's a life form."

"It may be," you say. "I'm getting sensations from it. It seems to be speaking softly, though not in words. Its mind is spread out. Its mind is in my mind, or my mind is in it!"

"I sense that too," says Nick.

"It seems to be thinking for me, and with me," you say. "I'm becoming part of it.

Nick"—you're calling him by name for the last time—"we are no longer who we were. We're part of a larger mind."

The End

Trillions upon trillions upon trillions of microscopic particles are spewing out of a white hole into a universe other than your own, the particles that once made up you among them.

The End

When you wake up, you're back in your space-ship, and everything that happened since you entered the black hole seems as if it were a dream: traveling through apple green space, past the smooth gray planets, then through the thick clay surface of the Earth-size planet. Strangest of all is your memory of the inside-out world beneath the surface, with its fields of lavender moss and multicolored plants, its upside-down mountains and amber-colored sky.

You glance at Nick, sitting at his station.

"Nick, how long have you been awake?"

"Just a few minutes," he says. "I've been try-ing to figure out whether we went through the black hole or I just dreamed it."

"I think we went through it," you say. "Unless we both dreamed it."

"I can't get over what we experienced," Nick says. "So weird."

"It sure was. Right now I'm worried about getting home."

Looking about, you recognize some familiar constellations. You take bearings on their princi-pal stars and feed the data into the computer. A few seconds later your screen lights up. You let out a cheer.

"Nick, the computer says we're only forty light-years from Earth!"

"That's not much help," he says. "Look at number three monitor. We're completely out of fuel!"

"We'll have to think of how to convert part of the ship into energy," you say.

Nick looks at you strangely. "Yes, I'm sure we can do that."

You feel sure of it too, because you're guided by the mind of Marabou!

You stand up and stretch your arms and legs. It will be good to be back on Earth again and see your family and friends.

You go to the bathroom and look in the mirror. You look well rested—very strong and healthy, in fact. But there is something a little different about your face. It looks smoother, almost better formed than you remember. You recognize yourself—there's no doubt that you are you—and yet you are no longer just you, you are more than you! It's too soon to tell what that means exactly. But it will mean many things for the future, of that you are sure, for within your mind is the mind of Marabou.

Turn to page 92.

Earth—Six Months Later

You're feeling a little numb, just as you did when you realized that you had woken up in another universe, but for a very different reason. The president of the Earth Federation has just shaken hands with you. He's pinning something on your jacket. He shakes hands again and says, "I am pleased to award you the Medal of Supreme Achievement." He reads the citation:

"For highest measure of courage and resourcefulness in passing through a black hole, visiting another universe, and returning safely again to your own universe, galaxy, star system, and to planet Earth."

Then a band is playing, everyone is smiling, and—you don't know how you know it, but there is no doubt in your mind—somewhere in another universe the mind of Marabou is smiling too.

The End

You are awake again, and so is Nick. You check around and are glad to see that you are on the *Athena*. It's cruising along, all functions working normally. You look through the view ports and check the monitors. Galaxies are visible in all directions, but no stars—you're clearly in intergalactic space.

"What an amazing level of science they have on Marabou," Nick says. "Somehow they got us through the white hole and back to our own universe."

"I hope it's our own universe," you say. "Nothing looks familiar."

"All sensors are giving normal readings," Nick says. "Whatever universe we're in must have the same rules of physics as ours."

"Computer analysis!" you practically shout, though the computer can hear a whisper that would be inaudible to human ears. "Conduct comparison of the universe atlas for observed galaxy patterns in our vicinity."

The data bank is so vast that even at picosecond speeds it takes the computer almost an hour to report. It's a report you hoped you'd never get.

The mind of Marabou transported you to another universe, but it's not your own.

Now your only hope is to find an Earth-like planet in the universe you're in. There's not much chance of that—you have only enough fuel to travel a few trillion miles, which in the vastness of space is like trying to find a place to stay overnight when there are none in sight and you can take only a few short steps.

The End

You set course for the planet Nicron. The computer reports that it's only twenty-three billion miles away. You should reach it in a few days.

"Search the data file," Nick says. "I know a probe was received from there once."

You're already asking the computer to scan its memory.

"Yeah, we have quite a bit of information about Nicron. It's similar to Earth. It has a moon, and it's just the right distance from its sun."

"Sounds good," Nick says. "Someone told me that it was almost a perfect planet, with plenty of food and resources, forests and lakes—everything we could want!"

"I heard that too," you say. "I also heard it's not a good place to live."

"How come?" Nick says.

The answer comes up on the screen:

Nicron is a perfect planet. It has every resource to be found on Earth, and no pollution. However, all spaceships are advised to stay away from it. Nicron's sun is likely to go supernova sometime in the next 50 years.

You and Nick exchange glances. You both know that a supernova is the explosion of a

massive star at the end of its normal life. No planet within a few light-years of such a cataclysm can survive.

"We could still hang out there for a while," Nick says.

You look at him skeptically, then nod.

"Better than floating around in space, I suppose."

The End

It's just a hunch of yours that the planet you're headed toward is hollowed out. But the more you think about it, the more your theory makes sense.

"Let's try to burrow into this planet," you tell Nick. "I'd rather try something desperate than drift through space until we run out of oxygen."

"You're the captain," says Nick, giving instructions to the computer.

You watch the planet growing larger as the *Athena* races toward it. Its surface looks more and more like clay.

Meanwhile, your computer is continually applying added power to maintain speed. There's no question now that reverse gravity increases as you get closer to an object, just as regular gravity does in your own universe.

"It might be too strong for us to penetrate, even with full power," Nick says.

You do some fast calculations. "I think we can make it. We should be able to hit the surface at close to a hundred miles an hour."

"Let's hope that gravity doesn't start pulling us down, the way it does in our own universe," Nick says. "We'd be wiped out."

You nod. "That's a chance we have to take, along with a lot of others. One good thing: If we get stuck in the planet's surface, the reverse gravity will help us get out."

You settle yourselves into crash positions. The *Athena* is designed to withstand a hundred-mile-an-hour impact, but will you be able to burrow through the planet's surface? And if so, what will you find inside?

About a mile from the surface, reverse gravity becomes so strong that you have to apply full emergency power. It's a strange feeling—diving at full speed toward ground that's trying to fling you back into space!

The altimeter is ticking off the distance to the planet's surface.

Nick catches your eye. "We're not going to make it," he says.

"I was thinking that too," you say.

The ship hits the ground, jostling you in your seats. The view ports are blacked out as you tunnel into the soft, claylike substance. You keep your eyes on the instruments.

"We're still alive," Nick says.

"Reduce power by half," you say. "The repulsion force is declining."

"But the clay is getting denser," Nick says. "It's slowing us down."

You glance at the data display. The ship is several hundred yards beneath the surface.

Suddenly the thruster output needles drop to zero.

"We've lost power," Nick says. "Clay must have seeped into the valves."

The *Athena* is still coasting, but it's slowing down. Nick looks frightened. He says the words that are in your mind.

"We may be trapped here forever."

The ship comes to a stop. You and Nick stare at each other.

"I would rather have floated in space forever," you say, "though I suppose it doesn't make any difference."

"There's one hope," Nick says. "The computer reports that our reverse thrusters aren't jammed. If they still work, we could back out the way we came in."

"If we're going to do that, we better try soon. The longer we wait, the more likely clay will seep into those valves too."

"Shall we try it?" says Nick.

Attempt to back out of the planet, turn to page 112.

*Take the time to consider other options,
turn to page 116.*

"I don't think we'll survive by crashing into a planet," you say.

"Okay," Nick says. "Then let's cruise around and see what else we can find."

You scan the area on your computer screen.

Nick taps your shoulder. "What's that on number three screen—thirty degrees to the right, fifteen vertical?"

"Probably a comet. The objects beyond it look like meteors. They could be debris from our own universe that fell into the black hole and came out on this side."

"The odds against anything surviving that are tremendous," Nicks says. "For every one we see, a million other objects must have been crushed in the singularity."

"That shows how strong that black hole is," you say. "It moves through space like a giant vacuum cleaner. Most things get stuck in the dust bag, but a few get through. We were extremely lucky."

"At least this gives us hope that other things exist in this universe. We might find something better to land on than these smooth gray spheres."

"Even if one were just like Earth, we'd still

have a problem. If we tried to walk around, reverse gravity would pull us up into space."

"We'd have to find caves to live in," Nick says. "Then we could walk on the ceiling."

You continue to cruise through the apple green space. You pass stray planets and asteroids, a couple of dwarf stars, and other debris, but not a single livable planet. You're beginning to feel discouraged when Nick jumps out of his seat.

"Over there!" He points out the starboard view port at an object that looks like a gigantic flying whale! It must be half a mile long, or even more, and it keeps opening and closing a mouth that takes up almost half its length.

"There's another one," you say, "and more behind them."

Investigate the giant objects, turn to page 145.
Keep away from them, turn to page 104.

You order the computer to take the *Athena* away from the giant objects. Even as your ship is turning and accelerating, one of them peels off from the others and comes after you.

The *Athena* responds to your command and accelerates out of reach. The space whale—for that's as close a name that you can think of to describe it—gives up the chase.

"That was a close one," Nick says. "This is a dangerous universe."

"Like our own," you say, slowing the *Athena* to cruising speed.

"What's that?" Nick exclaims, pointing to screen two, which shows a spiral form giving off bright yellow light.

"Let's take a closer look."

The *Athena* streaks toward the strange object. Though you're approaching it faster than the speed of light in your own universe, you don't seem to be getting closer.

"It must be very far away, and of stupendous size," you say. "Otherwise, it would seem to get bigger as we approach it."

A buzzer sounds. You look at screen two.

Fuel pump failure. Not remediable.

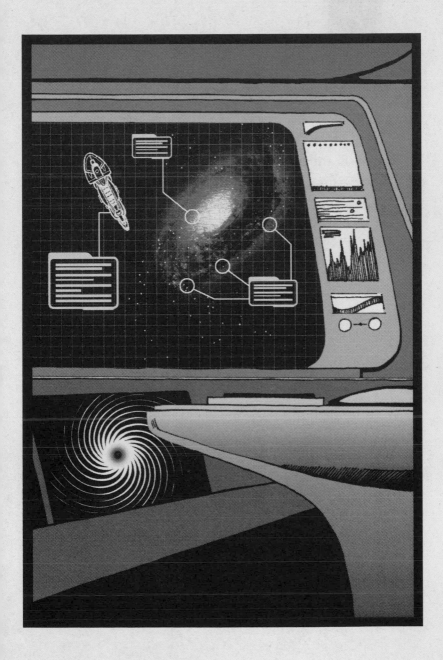

You and Nick exchange glances. Your engine has quit, so you're coasting at what is about one million miles a second in your new universe, headed toward a gigantic cavern three hundred trillion miles away. You'll get there in about ten years—nine and a half years after your oxygen runs out.

The End

You read the message on the screen over and over, but you could read it forever and it would still say the same thing.

"Nick," you say. "That was our last chance."

Hours pass, then days pass, and your hope fades. Your spaceship is trapped forever in the claylike crust of a nameless planet in a nameless universe somewhere beyond the black hole.

The End

You cruise toward home, but with the hatch cover missing and the cabin depressurized, there's no possibility of going into hibernation. Your oxygen supply can't last more than a few weeks—enough to travel forty billion miles. There are thousands of Earth ships traveling in space, but only a one-in-a-million chance that one will notice you.

The days pass. You are traveling at tremendous speeds, but the stars ahead of you don't seem to get any closer. You and Nick rarely say anything to each other. It would take too much energy, too much oxygen.

Finally it comes: the low, repeating beep that means you have three more hours of oxygen left. Now all you can do is wait for the end.

Your head begins to ache. You feel increasingly dizzy. Your brain goes numb.

You sense that you're coming back to consciousness. You're alive . . . and you're on another spaceship! A familiar figure is standing over your bunk. It's Lian Lee—you knew her at the academy!

"Lian . . . am I dreaming?"

"You're not," she says, smiling down on you. "You're on the *Liberty*. Command decided we should follow you as an extra backup. We were lucky to reach you in time."

"How's Nick?"

"He's fine," Lian says. "No sign of the *Nimrod*, though."

"They're lost," you say. "We picked up their beamer. They had a power failure and were pulled into the black hole."

Lian shakes her head. "We were afraid that's what happened."

After a while she says, "I guess you'll be glad to get back to Earth."

"Yeah," you say. "But I'm not through trying. Someday I'm going to go through the black hole."

The End

After typing in the code, you and Nick have only a ten-second warning to get into your cushioning restraints before you suddenly feel as if you weigh six hundred pounds, and that's what you're feeling now—too much for you to remain conscious.

When you come to—you're almost surprised that you do come to—you look over at Nick, who is just beginning to stir, then out the view port at stars and galaxies that look a lot like ones you saw as you were approaching the black hole.

You ask the computer to give you the ship's position. When you hear it, you let out a cheer. The antigravity generator not only got you away from the terrible pull of the black hole, but took you halfway to Earth. You'll have plenty of fuel to get the rest of the way.

Your first steps back on Earth are as wobbly as a toddler's, but you're smiling happily at the hundreds of people waiting to greet you and Nick.

Dr. Bartok is the first to walk up to you. You already radioed in a report, and you were afraid he would be critical of you for failing to make it through the black hole. Instead he shakes your hand warmly.

"You didn't get through the black hole," he says, "but because of your work we know a lot more about them than we did before. And you and Nick tested the antigravity generator and proved that in the presence of a very strong gravitational field it will work! You two are heroes!"

The End

"Nick," you say. "Let's get out of here." You activate the reverse thrusters and increase power.

Nothing happens.

"Keep increasing power," Nick says.

"I don't think we should," you say. "We might break loose so fast it would be impossible to control the ship."

"Ease power the second we're loose," Nick says.

You keep applying pressure on the reverse thrusters.

The engines are straining. Their high-pitched whine carries through the skin of the ship. Suddenly you're moving. The *Athena* reverses rapidly toward the outer surface of the planet. You ease the throttles. A half second later there is an explosive sound in the thrusters—something like a hugely amplified cough.

You're thrown back in your restraints as the ship brakes to a stop.

Nick hunches over the computer, trying to discover what happened.

"Ask for a contamination scan," you say.

Nick keys in instructions.

The data appears:

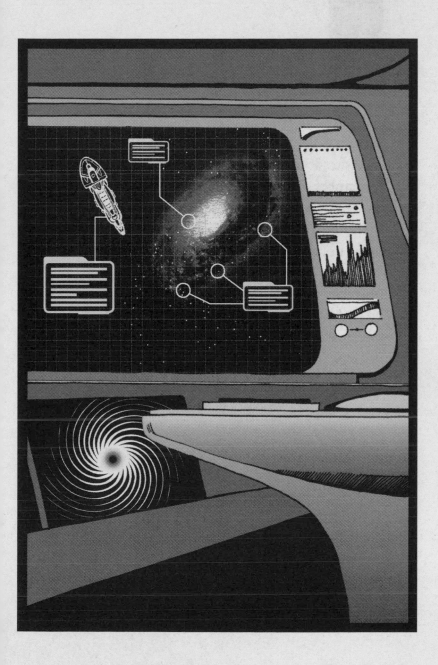

Reverse thrusters are jammed.

"Now all our thrusters are jammed. Anything we can do?" Nick asks.

You slowly shake your head, but then you remember that the *Athena* is equipped with an antigravity generator. Dr. Bartok said that it should be used only in the vicinity of a black hole, but that was in your own universe.

The question is, How would it work in a universe that has antigravity instead of gravity? Would it be a gravity generator? What would the effect of that be?

It's impossible to know, but maybe, just maybe, it would get you out of here.

Type in the computer code for the antigravity generator, continue to page 115.

Try to think what else to do, turn to page 116.

You successfully activate the antigravity generator, but don't live long enough to see what happens.

The End

"Let's think a moment," you say. "If we try to back out of here, we'll have to start from a dead stop. We're almost sure to get stuck in the clay."

"I wonder how far we are from the inner surface," Nick says.

"Wait a second."

You ask the computer for a density analysis of the clay ahead of the ship. A few seconds later it reports:

Infinite density.

Nick laughs. "That's its way of saying it can't figure things out in this universe," he says. "Let's try an ultrasonic probe."

"Good thinking."

It takes a moment for the UP screen to light up. You position the pointer, touch a button, and shoot an ultrasonic beam ahead of the ship. You and Nick watch the squiggly waves that appear on the monitor.

The pattern of sound waves changes when they reach the inner surface of the planet. In a moment a digital reading appears:

Distance to discontinuity: 3.7 meters.

"We're almost there!" Nick shouts.

"What luck!" You run over to shake his hand. The inner surface is about twelve feet away!

Nick's smile fades. "We're still going to have to tunnel through that stuff."

"We can cut a tunnel that far with the jets on our space suits."

Nick has a blank look on his face. You know he must be calculating something in his head. In a moment he says:

"Judging by how thick the clay is, it should take about an hour."

"We can carry enough oxygen for that," you say.

"I guess so," Nick says. "Maybe we'll reach the inner surface. But then what? There's not much chance we'll be able to stay alive once we're there."

"Maybe not," you say. "But there wasn't much chance we'd get this far—and yet we did. So let's get started!"

You blast open the hatch, using enough force to make a little crater in the thick, sticky clay that surrounds the spaceship. You and Nick crawl through and take turns directing blasts from your jet packs. The heavy, gooey material melts from the heat of your jets, leaving a hole that allows you to crawl a few inches more.

Foot by foot, yard by yard, you and Nick take turns crawling and blasting your way through the clay. You have several feet more to tunnel through when Nick's fuel runs out.

Now it's up to you alone.

You blast a little more clay and move forward. *It can't be much farther now,* you think. You blast again and gain a few more inches. Then your jet pack quits, out of fuel, like Nick's.

There's no way you can dig through this stuff without a blaster. You lie in the tunnel, trying to paw your way for the last few feet.

Nick is next to you. He shines a light back toward the *Athena.*

"The pressure of this stuff is squeezing the tunnel behind us." There's fear in his voice. "The clay starts closing the moment we open a passageway."

"Like those self-sealing tires," you say.

"With no jet pack fuel left we'll never get back to our spaceship."

You claw at the wall of clay.

"Don't panic," Nick says.

But you are panicked, and so is Nick. The sea of clay is closing in on the two of you. You keep clawing like a crazed animal. Your right arm feels weak. You claw with your left hand, again and again. You feel nothing in your fingers. They're free, in the open. You've reached the inner surface!

You manage to widen the hole enough to crawl through. In a moment you and Nick are both standing on stable ground.

You're both exhausted and covered with the congealed, claylike substance. Your jet packs are useless. Your food supplies are almost gone. You take off your helmet and try to breathe. No problem! You're breathing oxygen-rich air! The temperature is quite warm. You shed your mud-caked space suits.

You're a lot more comfortable in the work-out suits you're wearing underneath.

You're thinking what tremendous good luck it is that you can breathe the air and that this sticky clay hardens when exposed to it. But neither Nick nor you are talking. You're trying to make sense out of what's around you.

The ground under your feet is covered with

a sort of moss that must grow on the gray shell of the planet.

In some places hard rock protrudes above the surface. You guess it's made of the same substance as the gooey clay you tunneled through, and that it bulged out and then hardened when exposed to the air.

The land around you reminds you somewhat of Earth. There are no trees, but there are giant plants, many of them much taller than you.

Some look like enormous tulips and have huge red and yellow flowers that flutter in the breeze twenty feet above the ground. The stems and leaves of the plants are yellow and orange, the moss beneath your feet is a delicate shade of lavender. You can't figure out where the light comes from. There's no sun visible—just a soft, clear glow.

You crane your neck upward, turning to see in all directions. The sky is amazing, except that there is really no sky, or any horizon at all, because the land in the distance—beyond the tall plants and the low hills—curves slowly upward until it arches directly overhead. High in the sky is a range of rocky mountains that point down at you! Near the highest peaks—where, on Earth,

snow might lie—are patches of green, perhaps green ferns.

Another part of the sky is an almost-clear amber color and seems perfectly smooth. It could be a desert, or even an ocean.

"It's a beautiful world," Nick says. "And the air is fresh and pure."

"That's lucky," you say, "because I don't think we'll be able to leave it."

"Shhh!" Nick grabs your arm. "Look to the left."

On a sloping plain a few hundred yards away you see a group of very tall, yellowish, two-legged creatures. They look birdlike, except that they are furry rather than feathered, and have no wings.

"Don't move," you whisper to Nick. "Let's see what they do."

You watch as they move slowly across the plain, stopping from time to time to feed from plants growing up from the moss. A few of the larger ones bring up the rear. They seem to be guardians of the others, often stopping to sniff the air and look around.

One of the smaller ones runs off to the side. A big one makes a clicking sound. The little one stops short, then bounds back toward the group. You watch, fascinated, as they climb the hill beyond the meadow and disappear over the crest.

"They were worried about something," Nick says.

"They're at least eight feet tall," you say. "If there are predators around, they must be pretty big."

You and Nick look around cautiously. You see some big, lazy-looking insects flitting around the flowering plants, but no other animal life.

"We've got to find a source of food," Nick says. "Do you think we should take a look at the plants those animals were eating? They must be all right for us. Or look for water first?"

Inspect the plants, turn to page 124.
Look for water, turn to page 127.

You and Nick reach the meadow where the bird-like creatures were feeding. You soon find the object of their attention: low, bushy plants loaded with big, juicy fruit that reminds you of grapes.

They're all over the place, and most of them haven't been touched. You're wary of eating plants—you would never try a strange berry back on Earth. But there's no other food in sight. You pick one and sniff it. You touch it with your tongue, then bite off a piece of it. It's good. Very good.

"I think it's okay," you tell Nick.

He tries one, and then another. "They're not just okay," he says. "They're great."

"Just eat one," you say. "Then wait awhile to make sure we can digest them."

But Nick is biting at a third one. "Nothing that tastes this good can be bad for you," he says. "I didn't realize how hungry I was!"

You're hungry too, and you eat another. What luck this is! They're the best-tasting fruit you have ever eaten.

Nick and you are so happy eating the fruit you've found that you forget about the predators that the bird creatures were watching for.

You don't hear them until they are almost on

top of you: great, bearlike creatures with huge jaws and teeth like spikes. They are slow and clumsy—you could have outrun them if you had seen them in time.

You enjoyed eating the fruit, but not as much as the spike-toothed bears enjoy eating you.

The End

"It's more important to find water," you say.

"It's a long way to that water." Nick points upward, to where the sky would be if you were on Earth. Because you are standing on the planet's inner surface, he's pointing not at the sky, but at the other side of the world!

"Nick, we don't even know if that is water, or even if water exists in this universe. We haven't seen a cloud."

"Yet it doesn't feel dry. It's got to rain here," he says, "or there wouldn't be plants."

"Maybe it rains at night."

Nick looks at you strangely. "I have a feeling it's always daytime here."

Green and yellow butterflies flitter past. Their colors are so beautiful that they seem to give off their own light! They hover nearby, like tiny helicopters. A clear, musical voice fills the air.

You will find water in the hollows of amber vines. You may eat plants or berries that are orange, red, or yellow. Do not eat anything else. Watch for the spike-toothed bears. Sleep and rest on lavender moss. Do not cross a river that flows over pink sand.

You and Nick stare at each other in disbelief. You can't tell where the voice is coming from. It seemed to come from the butterflies.

"Who are you? Where are you?" you shout. The answer comes back: *We are the mind of Marabou.*

"What does that mean?" Nick says.

There is no answer. The butterflies disappear, like a vanishing multicolored cloud.

Nick points after them. "*That* was the mind of Marabou."

You and Nick wander inside the hollow planet for three days and three nights, except that, as Nick suspected, there are no nights. The amber-colored sky is always clear. When you get tired, you sleep on lavender moss.

In your travels you see many strange creatures and many beautiful plants. You find water in the hollows of the amber vines. It tastes like cold, clear springwater. The fruits you eat are better than any you've eaten on Earth.

Occasionally you see spike-toothed bears. They often start toward you, but they are very slow, and you have no trouble outrunning them. Once you reach the lavender moss, you're safe. They won't step on it.

A fourth day's travel brings you to a river that blocks your way. It doesn't look deep or dangerous.

The water is exceptionally clear. The bottom

is made of pink sand. It's not more than twenty yards wide. The current is running at a moderate pace.

"I guess we have to turn back," Nick says.

"We can wade across," you say. "We can turn back if it gets too deep or the current gets too fast."

"The mind of Marabou warned us against it."

"We've got to find someone we can talk to, someone who can help us," you say. "Maybe there's something across the river that the mind of Marabou doesn't want us to know—something that could help us."

"Maybe," Nick says. "But are you sure we should chance it?"

Stick to this side of the river, turn to page 135.

Wade in a little ways and decide for yourself whether it's safe to cross the river, turn to page 142.

"Nick, I think we should stay where we are," you say. "It was a miracle that we got here in the first place. It would take about ten miracles to get back to our own universe."

"I feel the same way," Nick says.

"Tell me, Caru . . . ," you start to say, but the alien is gone!

You and Nick look at each other helplessly. "I don't think we'll see Caru again," you say. "He—they—must have decided we don't need more help."

"*I* think we need help," Nick says.

At that moment a three-foot-tall sunflower rises up out of the clay.

"My gosh," Nick exclaims. "It's as if anything can happen here."

Not anything, a voice, seeming to come from the sunflower, says.

"Nick, I think the mind of Marabou is back." You can't help smiling.

"Hello," you say to the sunflower, though you feel a little silly doing so.

"Can you help us?" Nick says.

Can you help us? the sunflower says. *We want to make this a perfect planet, and you may have some ideas that will help us, things you've learned on your own planet.*

"I'm not sure how much help we'd be," you say. "Earth is a very imperfect planet."

Then perhaps you can tell us what not to do.

Say you'll help, continue to page 133.

*Say you don't think you'd be any help,
turn to page 134.*

"We'll help as best we can," you say.

"We'll make a list of things," Nick says. "Like cars, roads, computers, houses . . ." His voice trails off. The sunflower is curling over a little, as if it's beginning to wilt.

Why not start telling us what's imperfect about your planet? the sunflower says.

You think a moment before replying, "What's imperfect is the problems humans have, like greed and cruelty. If we didn't have these, Earth might be a perfect planet too."

Thank you, the sunflower says. *We'll make sure we have no greed or cruelty on Marabou, only kindness and fun.*

"If you can achieve that," you say, "this will be the best planet in your universe."

"In any universe," says Nick.

The End

"I don't think we can help you much," you say. "We don't come from a perfect planet, and I don't think we can help make this one perfect either."

The sunflower fades, then disappears, and you and Nick are left alone.

"Maybe I was too abrupt," you say.

"I'm wondering, can we even survive here?" Nick says.

"I think so. We have been told all we need to know. It may not be a perfect planet, but we'll live forever and never grow old."

Nick looks up at the amber-colored sky and at the upside-down mountains. "It is a beautiful place," he says, "but will we ever be happy if we never see another human?"

"I'm not sure," you say. "But I think we'll see other humans. We just have to be patient. Humans love to explore. Someday, I bet, they'll enter the black hole we came through and find us. If it's true, as the mind of Marabou said, that we'll never grow old, we'll be here to greet them."

The End

"I guess we better stay on this side of the river," you say. "Let's follow it upstream toward those hills."

"Look!" Nick is pointing off to the right.

Of all the odd things that you've seen since you passed through the black hole, none seems stranger than this: a very humanlike figure, who has appeared out of nowhere and now is walking toward you.

"This can't be," Nick says.

You nod. "We must be cracking up."

"Wh-who are you?" Nick blurts out.

The humanlike creature looks nice enough, with straight black hair and clear brown eyes. Yet there is something strange about the way he or she—or it—walks, and about the shape of the face, as if it were molded from plastic.

"Caru," the figure says in a pleasant voice.

"Who are you? Did you come from Earth?" Nick asks.

"We look like you Earth people while talking to you, but we are very different. We are the mind of Marabou."

"Like the butterflies?"

The figure nods. "We have assumed a form like yours so we can communicate in a friendlier way."

"You said 'we.' Are you one person or many?"

"Both," Caru says. "In a way you could not understand."

"What do you mean when you say you're the mind of Marabou?" Nick asks.

The figure raises a finger. A lightning bolt streaks across the sky! Caru's hands come together. Thunder rumbles over the valley! The creature's hands fall to its sides, and all is still.

Nick's jaw is hanging open. "You're some kind of god!"

"Or magician," you add.

Caru smiles. "We are neither a god nor a magician. Everything we have achieved is through science."

You step in and study the alien's face.

"But how . . . how do you know we're from Earth? How can you speak our language?

"We scanned your computer's memory. It contains the record of your flight and much information about you and your home universe."

"You dug through the tunnel to our spaceship?"

"There was no need to dig," Caru replies. "We scan metaelectronically."

The alien sits on a patch of lavender moss

and crosses its legs. "In this body we find it more comfortable to sit than stand. You may sit too, if you like."

Nick walks up to Caru. "Are you an android?" he asks.

Caru laughs. "No, we are not an android any more than we are a god or a magician. An android can only do what it is programmed to do. The body we are in is like that of an android, but that is only a temporary convenience. We can place our mind anywhere."

"There are many things we don't understand about this universe," Nick says. "Out in space it seemed to us that gravity repelled instead of attracted. But somehow it's holding us here on the ground. We feel almost as heavy here as we do on Earth."

"It is not gravity that holds you to the ground," Caru says. "It's the antigravity of the white star in the center of this planet."

"What do you mean?" you say, looking up overhead. "I don't see a star."

"You can't see it," Caru says, "because it's only a few inches across. It's a tiny white hole in the cosmos. It is the repulsive force of the tiny white hole that hollowed out this planet. This same force keeps you from rising up in the air. Its energy provides the light by which we see—though this is diffused rather than coming from one point."

"This is hard to understand," Nick says.

Caru smiles. "That's because it's the opposite of what you're used to. If you had been born here and visited Earth, you would find it peculiar to be living on the outside surface of a planet. You would probably grab hold of a tree to keep from flying off into space."

While Caru is talking, you are looking straight up toward the white star. All you can see, though, is the other side of the planet, the upside-down mountains and the amber-colored sky. An idea strikes you.

"Caru, is there any way we could journey through that white hole and get back to our own universe?"

Caru nods. "We are in the process of building a perfect planet here. It will be filled with wonderful creatures and plants—a few of them you have already seen. If you stayed here, you would be able to learn and do things you could never do on Earth or anywhere else in your own universe. You could live forever and never grow old.

"We understand why you would want to

return home, and we will do our best to help you, but we must warn you that though we are far more advanced than earthlings, there are limits to what we can do. We could easily pass through a black hole, as you did to get here, but in this universe there are no black holes—only white holes.

"To enter a black hole, one need only dive into it. White holes are more of a problem. The closer you get, the harder they push you away. Even with engines a million times stronger than anything on Earth, you could not push hard enough to enter a white hole."

Nick has a mournful expression on his face. "It looks as if we're stuck here," he says.

Caru holds up one hand. "There is one chance. Just as we can organize our atoms and subatoms into those of a humanlike person or a swarm of butterflies, we could organize your atoms into another shape."

"But we'd still be repelled, wouldn't we?" Nick asks.

Caru smiles. "Not if the mind of Marabou transformed you into negative particles. Instead of being repelled, they would be drawn into the white hole and then emerge as particles in your own universe. There they would transform into their original state—meaning you."

"That's far beyond any science we have on Earth," Nick says, "but after what I've seen, I don't doubt you can do it."

"Even if you could do this," you say, "and we were able to emerge again in our own universe, wouldn't we find ourselves just floating through space?"

"No," says Caru. "Because we would transmit not only you, but also your spaceship!"

"I don't see how we'd make it all the way home," you say. "Besides, our ship is stuck in the clay, and it's almost out of fuel."

Caru, nodding, simply says, "You will be able to do much that you could not do before."

"What do you mean?"

The strange alien fastens a hypnotic gaze upon you. "We shall impart to you the mind of Marabou."

These ideas make you dizzy. Nick looks like they make him even dizzier.

"What do you think?" he asks you.

Try to return to your own universe through the white hole, turn to page 151.

Stay where you are, turn to page 131.

"Let's see," you say.

You wade in up to your shins.

Nick, staring at the water, says nothing.

You step back and pick up a stick by the river-bank, toss it in midstream, and watch it float gently along with the current.

"The river's not that deep, and look at that stick," you say. "We could swim faster than the current if we had to."

"Okay," Nick says. "Let's try it, but you first."

You start wading across the river. Nick follows. Even when you reach midstream, the water is only up to your hips. The current is flowing at its fastest here, but there's no danger of being swept off your feet.

You take a few more steps. Already the water is getting shallower! You half turn and look back. "Come on, Nick—I'm almost ac—" You never finish the sentence. Dagger teeth have sunk into your leg. You look down and realize why you didn't see it sooner: The crocodile-like creature that's tearing your leg off is the same pink color as the river-bottom sand.

"Nick, get back!" you scream.

The End

You instruct the computer to head the *Athena* directly into the black hole. You're almost certain to be crushed by tidal forces before you reach the singularity, the point where thousands of stars and planets have already been compressed into nothingness. But there's a chance—just a chance—that you'll reach the point where the rules of physics no longer apply, where you'll find a wormhole to another universe.

The blackness opens up before you. It is surrounded by a ghostly purple glow, the light of millions of stars, their strange colors caused by the relativistic effects.

Nick seems frozen at his computer. For a second you think time may have stopped, then realize that it didn't. For one thing, you're still thinking.

You're thinking that this hope of yours to get through the black hole is totally fanciful, that now is the time to activate the antigravity generator and escape from the hole's terrible pull. There are just two reasons not to: One is that you can't be sure it won't malfunction and destroy the ship, and with it, you and Nick. The other reason is that it would be shirking the duty you took on: to try to get through the black hole despite the risks involved.

But do you have such a duty when it would almost be like suicide to try? One thing is sure: You've got to make your decision now!

Type in 3.1415 as the computer code of the antigravity generator, turn to page 110.

Continue trying to get through the black hole, turn to page 150.

Quantum divergence.

Turn to either page 146 or page 147.

You steer the *Athena* toward the closest gigantic flying whale. It's about thirty times as big as your spaceship and it looks dangerous, but the *Athena* can travel thousands of times faster than a whale. You can easily outrun it if it chases you.

So you think! But this is not a whale, it's a whalelike creature. It's not in an ocean, it's in space. And it's not in your own universe, it's in a very different one. You realize this as the creature's incredibly enormous teeth crunch down on the *Athena*'s hull.

The End

You take a moment to look out the other view port. One of the creatures is coming straight at you!

"Full power!" you scream at Nick.

The *Athena* accelerates, like a small fish that barely manages to swim free of the jaws of a whale.

The alien monster veers off, looking for easier prey.

You and Nick stare at each other, shaken by how close you came to extinction.

Soon you've left the school of monsters far behind you. You're feeling good until a message comes up on your screen:

Fuel supply will be exhausted in 120 seconds.

Nick looks up from his screen and says, "Since we're traveling at infinite speed, that's enough time for us to travel an infinite distance."

"Very funny, Nick."

But it's not funny. Nick was just reminding you that the computer produces weird results because of the different laws of physics here.

The *Athena* is still racing at an incredible speed through the green-hued space of another universe. Computer controls are frozen. The screen gave you a message, but you can't control the ship.

Ahead of you is a great rose-colored object shaped like an enormous open mouth. You can't see what lies beyond it, or within it, but the *Athena* is being pulled toward it.

You and Nick sit helplessly at the controls. You don't think you'll be alive more than a few minutes more.

You feel yourself losing consciousness. . . .

You and Nick are alive and awake, sitting on lounge chairs by a tropical lagoon. Birds are singing; butterflies are fluttering through the air; sweet music is playing in your ears; happy thoughts are running through your brain. Soon you will learn more about where you are and what experiences you will have, ones that you could never have imagined, arranged by an intelligence more advanced than any in your universe.

The End

You are inside the event horizon, past the point of no return, even for light itself. Somewhere ahead is the singularity.

The *Athena* falls deeper into the darkness.

Your name, along with Nick's, is engraved on a brass plaque next to the main entrance to Space Academy. You will be remembered as one of the great space explorers, through you never made it through the black hole.

The End

"This is a beautiful planet," you say to Nick, "but I don't want to stay here forever. I'm willing to take a chance on making it home."

"So am I," he says.

"You are brave," Caru says. "We shall do what we can to help you succeed. Now take a last look around, because while you are transformed into another state, you will not be conscious. You will not even be able to dream."

Caru steps forward and shakes hand with you and Nick. Then it is as if you are sleeping a dreamless sleep, except for two weird words circling about in your mind: *Quantum divergence*.

Turn to either page 93 or page 89.

About the Author

Edward Packard conceived of the idea and wrote what became the prototype book for Bantam's classic Choose Your Own Adventure® series and wrote over sixty books in the series, several of which are available in revised and expanded form as U-Ventures® at the iTunes app store. Packard's latest book, *All It Takes—the Three Keys to Making Wise Decisions and Not Making Stupid Ones*, was published in 2011.